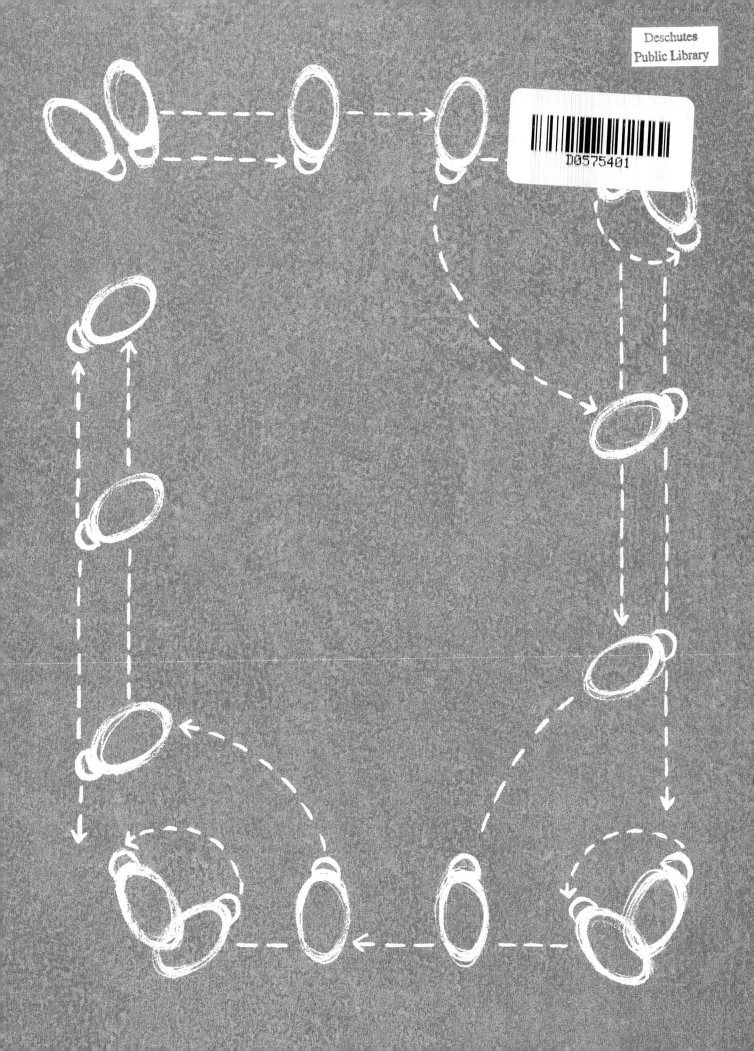

For all my little friends at Endeavor Hall Charter School —K. C.

To the Nerd Herd —M. I.

Text copyright © 2017 by Kristyn Crow
Illustrations copyright © 2017 by Molly Idle

First published in the United States of America in June 2017
by Bloomsbury Children's Books
www.bloomsbury.com

Bloomsbury is a registered trademark of Bloomsbury Publishing Plc

For information about permission to reproduce selections from this book, write to
Permissions, Bloomsbury Children's Books, 1385 Broadway, New York, New York 10018
Bloomsbury books may be purchased for business or promotional use. For information on bulk purchases please contact
Macmillan Corporate and Premium Sales Department at specialmarkets@macmillan.com

Library of Congress Cataloging-in-Publication Data
Names: Crow, Kristyn, author. | Idle, Molly Schaar, illustrator.
Title: Zombelina : school days / by Kristyn Crow ; illustrated by Molly Idle.
Other titles: School days
Description: New York : Bloomsbury, 2017.
Summary: The only thing Zombelina loves as much as dancing is going to school.
Zombelina has an idea to help her new friend work through his show-and-tell day jitters!
Identifiers: LCCN 2016032035 (print) | LCCN 2016050237 (e-book)
ISBN 978-1-61963-641-5 (hardcover) • ISBN 978-1-68119-473-8 (e-book) • ISBN 978-1-68119-474-5 (e-PDF)
Subjects: | CYAC: Stories in rhyme. | Zombies—Fiction. | Dance—Fiction. | Schools—Fiction. | Stage fright—Fiction. | Friendship—Fiction. |
BISAC: JUVENILE FICTION / Performing Arts / Dance. | JUVENILE FICTION / Family / General (see also headings under Social Issues). |
JUVENILE FICTION / School & Education. | JUVENILE FICTION / Social Issues / Friendship.
Classification: LCC PZ8.3.C8858 Zs 2017 (print) | LCC PZ8.3.C8858 (e-book) | DDC [E]—dc23
LC record available at https://lccn.loc.gov/2016032035

Art created with Prismacolor pencils on vellum-finish Bristol
Typeset in Oldbook ITC Std
Book design by Regina Flath and Yelena Safronova
Printed in China by Leo Paper Products, Heshan, Guangdong
1 3 5 7 9 10 8 6 4 2

All papers used by Bloomsbury Publishing, Inc., are natural, recyclable products made from wood grown in well-managed forests.
The manufacturing processes conform to the environmental regulations of the country of origin.

Zombelina
School Days

Kristyn Crow

illustrated by
Molly Idle

BLOOMSBURY
NEW YORK LONDON OXFORD NEW DELHI SYDNEY

It's me, Zombelina, all ready for school.
I finish my breakfast of lizard-eye gruel,
and check myself out in my daddy's X-ray.
My mom says, "You look drop-DEAD
gorgeous today!"

I leap on the school bus and
twirl down the aisle . . .

TWISTED TREE LN.

I swivel my hips, and I stretch out in style.

Today's show-and-tell day, and nobody knows,

my hip-hop's to DIE for! I break like the pros!

Ms. Roth says, "Good morning, class. Please take a seat.
We have a new student I'd like you to meet—
Morty just moved here."

We tell him, "Hello."
Then Morty slumps down in the very back row.

I sit beside Lizzie, my friend who's a dancer.
Whenever we do math, we BOTH like to answer.

"I know it!" I cry, with my hand in the air . . .

but it falls on the floor and rolls under the chair.

We work on our grammar and spelling, then read.
I find a new book and it's just what I need!

Ms. Roth is concerned. She comes over to look.

"Why, you really DO put your nose in a book!"

We're done reading books, so we put them away . . .
and that means it's now show-and-tell time! HURRAY!

Show and Tell: TALENTS!

We're sharing our talents. I know I'm prepared.
I've practiced my steps, and I'm not a bit scared.

Ramone shares his trophies.
There's artwork by Kate.

I stretch out my legs, and
I patiently wait.

"You're next, Zombelina."

I get up to dance . . .

then sway and sashay in a
weird zombie trance.

I snap dance and six-step and
scootbot to start.

But suddenly things begin falling apart.

I can't get a grip, and I'm losing control.
I hear a few whispers. My eyes start to roll.
My classmates are gasping.
No, this isn't good.
I hold it together like real dancers should.

I curtsy to finish, but nobody claps.

So I walk to my desk in a daze . . . and collapse.

Then Morty says, "My turn? Oh . . . maybe I'll sing.
I'm not very good at this show-and-tell thing."

His fingers are shaking. He stares at the floor.
I know how he feels—I've had stage fright before.
"Don't worry," I whisper, "you're gonna do fine.
There's no way your talent could go worse than MINE."

Show and Tell: TALENTS!

He nods and he quivers, then sings out of tune.

It's awesome! Like werewolves that howl at the moon!

A few kids are laughing and plugging their ears.

But Lizzie and I drown them out with our cheers.

Then later at recess,
he gives us a hug.
"You wanna go searching
to find a new bug?

I like to inspect them, and I need a bee."
I blink a few times. "That sounds perfect to me."

We play bug detective, and I find a clue!
Lizzie's creeped out, but she finds a few, too.

Morty says, "Most people tell me I'm strange.
It's nice to have good friends like YOU for a change."

We line up our bugs in a row on the ground.
Then . . . what's this? Our class starts to gather around.
"Zombelina, you're freaky," they say. "Morty, too.
And all of us wish we could hip-hop like you."

"Will you teach us those dance steps—before you were tangled?
Your dancing was dead on, until you got mangled."

I tell them to line up. We show them some moves.
Poor Morty keeps tripping. I hope he improves.

BRRRRRRRRrrrriiiiiiiiiIINNNNNGGG!

Awwwww. That's the bell. We were having such fun!
Wait—I have an idea! A FABULOUS one.
I whisper to Lizzie. She claps with delight!
Together, we plan out a DANCE-tastic night.

You're Invited to
Zombelina's
Back-to-School
DANCE PARTY!
1313 Twisted Tree Lane
7:00 p.m. Spine-chilling Saturday
Come GET YOUR GROOVE ON

I clear out the attic, put on my best tights.
My mom makes the snacks and
my dad works the lights.

My classmates arrive and my teacher does, too!
I show off some dance steps and teach them a few.

We moonwalk with mummies. We boogie with bats.
We wiggle with werewolves and rock out with rats!

We're each very different, but that makes us cool.
Now I'm DYING to see all my friends back at school.

And Morty's collections have started a trend.
So here's LIVING proof things turn out in . . .

The End

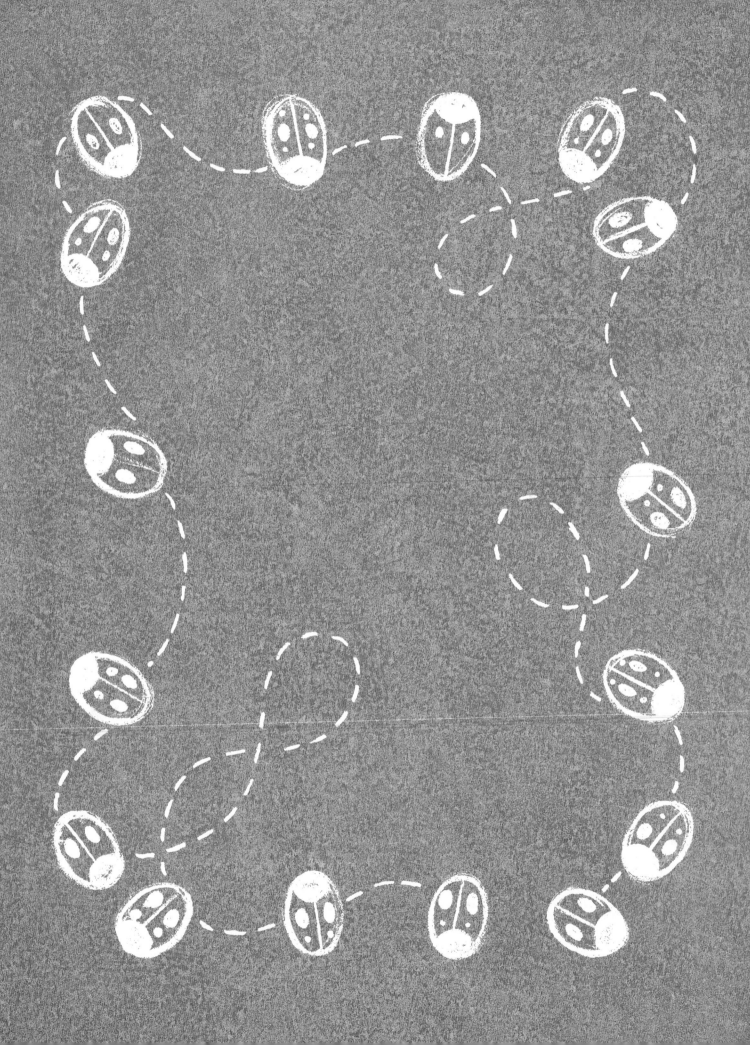